Grace's Euro Adventures

By Emma Drag

Grosvenor House
Publishing Limited

This book is published by
Grosvenor House Publishing Ltd
Link House
140 The Broadway, Tolworth, Surrey, KT6 7HT.
www.grosvenorhousepublishing.co.uk

A CIP record for this book
is available from the British Library

ISBN 978-1-80381-573-2

"You can never dream too big".

Rachael Blackmore
(first female Jockey to
win the Grand National, 2021)

To all children: aim high, dream big!

The Line Up

1 The warm-up   1
2 The Netherlands   19
3 Trip home   32
4 Italy   45
5 Out at the park   60
6 Germany   73
7 Stadium away-day   90
8 Northern Ireland   104
9 Planning the adventure with Beth   119
10 Arriving at Wembley – the final   128
11 The history of England's women's
   football   145

Note: factual female footballers' names correct at the time of writing.

Sue Lopez played for Southampton, played a season at Roma, and made 22 appearances for England Women's team – affectionately known as the Lionesses. Between 1966–1985 she played football. Sadly, she now has dementia, which she says is the result of years of heading the ball.

1

The warm-up

Football is Grace's life. Grace Tucker eats, sleeps and lives for the game. She takes after her mum Angela who, when she lived in Germany, was a professional sports woman. For 10-year-old Grace, school is fun because PE lessons involve team sports, including football. Football was brilliant fun for Grace in the winter months (that was the only time teachers taught football). In the winter, the ground was hard from the frost, and Grace liked making crunching sounds when running around the pitch. She liked seeing her warm breath in the cold air, and when the ball is being defended at the opposition's goal, she entertains herself by puffing out air like a steam engine. In the summer came the grand tournaments on TV.

Being slightly smaller than her school friends gave Grace a special set of advantages that helped her become a talented forward. She has the ability to dart between defenders and run around the opposition, like a dog waiting for its owner to throw the ball. Evenings and weekends would involve either practising, talking about or watching sport. Grace's dad, Phil, would take Grace to football while her mum would take her brother Benjamin to rugby.

"You're a girl. You really shouldn't be playing football," teased Benjamin, as Mum tied Grace's hair into a messy bun. Benjamin knew how to wind his sister up, and his silly faces were a step too far.

"Don't be mean to your sister, Benjamin. She has just as much right to play sport as you do," Dad piped up.

There always seemed to be these comments before football practice, and it was getting rather boring for Grace. It was everywhere, but it just made Grace want to play football more. She felt that football was really when she came alive and she could really do her best. Benjamin played rugby. Mum watched, but Grace just let him get on with it. Benjamin had Mum wrapped around his little finger. When he needed a new pair of boots or the latest rugby top, Mum bought it for him. Grace, however, was happy with the random gift of top, shorts and socks, and only asked for things if they were broken or she was growing out of them. Her football boots were plain and simple. They did the job.

At the front door, Grace's right hand picked up her red boot bag, and carried her water bottle patterned with her name in gold. With her boots and shin pads in her left hand, she followed Dad to their silver car. It was quite a journey to training but both Dad and Grace always felt it was worth it. It was a time they could play George Ezra and Dad's favourite U2 music and sing together in the car; a time to discuss tactics and what the end of training treat would be.

"How are you feeling about the last training session of the season, Grace?" Dad asked while Grace played on his mobile phone to get the next song on.

"Yeah, it should be fun, Dad," answered Grace. "I'll play forward then give someone else a go. I hope Sam doesn't get us running too much today!"

Grace couldn't find another song so she put on the local radio station, Estimate FM instead. Dad smiled as he drove and started tapping out the rhythm to *We will rock you* by Queen when it came on. "Perhaps Sam will get you to do a few two versus two games, just to practice the tackling," finished Dad.

Oaktree was a large town 35 minutes along the A-road from Marlbury, a small village where the Tucker family lived. Oaktree Fields Football Club is a respectful football team. They have teams from Little Strikers to the Women's and Men's senior teams, including a blind football team, a walking team, and a wheelchair team. The men's team were recently promoted and the ladies' team had just finished a successful first season in the women's premier league. Oaktree Fields FC were excited about the future, with a space for anyone who wanted to play.

"Hello, everyone," Sam the football coach began. "Tonight is the last week of training before the summer break. I'm sure you will be sad about that but there will be lots of football to enjoy this summer, with the Lionesses playing in the Euros."

"Hooray!" went the crowd of parents and 20 ten-year-olds.

As the training session began, the adults either went to the cafe or stood far away from the touchline to chat. Training commenced with a warm-up game called hills and valleys (some teachers may call it cups and saucers). Players got into two teams. Sam had put the cones out ready to start before the team arrived. Some of the cones were placed normally (the hills) and some were turned with the base facing upwards (the valleys). Sam gave the team 30 seconds to turn the cones to whichever team they were.

Suddenly the time ended. The whistle blew loud; the game stopped. Grace's best friend, Beth, cheekily turned a cone over but was spotted and was told to turn it back. The valley team won; they turned more cones over to look like valleys. The valley team cheered while the hill team had sad faces.

"Right, everyone," resumed the coach. "This time the hill team will turn the cones to show valleys and the valley team will turn the cones to show hills. Three, two, one, go."

The whistle blew and off they went to play their game. This time the hills team won. *To make everyone feel better*, Grace thought.

Grace became excited about the next part of the training session: the one versus two, and three versus two quick games. Grace always talked to Beth and her team about how these quick games helped to become accurate at passing, and how they should try to gain possession of the ball.

After a while, Grace heard the shrill sound of the whistle, and everyone gathered ready for a football game in which everyone joined in. Grace ran to the centre spot ready to kick the ball.

After 10 minutes of the whole team game, the players took a five-minute drink break and then played for a further 10 minutes. In the second half, Grace tried a different position (right-back) just to find out how she felt about defending.

Finally came the cooling down with a game of 'keeping the ball in the square'. Grace enjoyed this quick-paced game where you were out when you missed the ball.

Grace loved training, and by the start of the hills and valleys game, Benjamin's comments were history. Grace loved being a forward and enjoyed practising darting in and out of the opposition. She even went in goal so others could experience a different position. Grace was a team player. She was encouraging and able to give her friends advice. Dad said she would make a good captain one day.

An hour and a half flew by and the final whistle blew. Everyone gathered around Sam, who spoke about the final session and things to practise over the summer break. Training came to an end and the team said their goodbyes. Beth hugged Grace.

"See you at school tomorrow, Grace!" said Beth.

"Yes, of course. 'Bye, Beth," Grace replied as she picked up the water bottle off the emerald-green grass. As she looked at her boot bag, ready to pick it up, she could see an older lady walking slowly towards her.

"Hi, you are Grace aren't you?" spoke the lady softly.

How does she know my name? Grace thought.

"I'm Sue Lopez. I used to play football when I was younger – for Southampton and England."

Grace was shocked. "Hi, Sue. I've read so much about you. You were a forward like me!"

"Yes," smiled Sue. "I saw you playing as I came for my evening walk."

The pair walked across the pitch together and sat on the bench overlooking the Oaktree field.

"It must be getting towards the end of your season now." Sue began.

"Yes," replied Grace. "It's sad. I don't like finishing. It's more than two months without seeing everyone from the team.

"You are like I was. The girls and I always wanted to keep playing when we had free time." Sue paused and looked down at her bag. She took out a small photo album and turned over the cover. "There were lots of girls and women playing before me. This is Lily Parr", she said pointing to a photograph of a female player. "She played for St. Helens Ladies and then for Dick, Kerr Ladies. Dick, Kerr was a factory, and during World War One many factories, which were operated by women while the men were away, had their own football teams. Lily was mainly a left-winger."

Grace stared at the photos as Sue turned the pages and talked about how football was back then.

"Dick, Kerr Ladies were a great team and they played as the England team too. *Big* crowds watched them and they raised money for charity," Sue continued.

"That's really good," Grace said, smiling, enjoying being with Sue. "I like raising money for charity. Beth and I raised money for the Oaktree Fields football kit by selling our homemade biscuits and lemonade." They smiled at each other.

"Then in 1921, the England FA banned women's teams from all FA grounds. They said 'football is quite unsuitable to women'!" Sue and Grace looked at each other and they rolled their eyes. "But Lily Parr and her friends still played on any park or field they could find," Sue said, continuing the football story.

"I wonder if they played here." Grace looked around at the football pitches surrounded by the old, oak trees.

"Mmm, I wonder!" Sue replied, smiling at Grace.

"So, when did the FA allow women to play on the FA grounds?" Grace continued her questioning, thinking about how unfair this was and how she felt lucky to be in a town where football is for all.

"1971, but the women who went to play in the Mexico World Cup came home and were given a three-month ban!" Sue and Grace's faces turned from being happy to frowning.

"Anyway, Grace, your dad will be waiting at your car for you. It's been lovely talking to you, and keep playing!" Grace gave Sue a hug and thanked her for sharing the history of women's football.

"Oh, I almost forgot. Here, I want to give you this – a forward passing the key to the next forward." With that, Sue got up from the bench, turned, said, "Good luck!" and started to walk away from Grace.

Grace looked around to see if anyone had seen the two of them talking but there was no one. Grace looked at the key and wondered what Sue meant when she'd said good luck. Suddenly, the key began to shine. It was so bright; a brightness Grace had never seen before.

The key was rather old-fashioned. It had a long middle section, with one end shaped into a football boot that fingers would hold to turn the key to open a door, cupboard or a treasure box. The other end, a well-crafted but rather jagged section and well used. Grace wondered what it could be used for, especially these days when things are operated by buttons, apps and remotes!

Grace looked around again but no one was around her. Her dad was walking towards the car having presumed Grace had followed him.

As Grace picked up the water bottle, which she'd dropped when she took the key from Sue, her shamrock-coloured eyes were drawn to the goalmouth. The goal end looked rather hazy, and Grace began to slowly walk across to it to have a closer look. The goal was shimmering and sparkling just like the key. The area beyond the goal was twirling around and around. Grace could see that no one else had noticed what she was seeing. Everyone else was driving off in their cars, and Dad was still walking to theirs.

Grace rather nervously started walking faster towards the goalmouth.

As she got closer she noticed there was a door in front of her; an old-fashioned door, orange in colour with large bolts and a metal lock. The perfect door for this key. Grace looked around the goalmouth. By now the nets had been taken down and all that was left was the frame. Grace looked carefully before putting her hand through the space, just like a magician would ask a member of the audience to check a magic hat or the wardrobe for mysterious pockets or hidden exits. Grace grew excited about the door and tried the key, now shimmering orange in colour. The key slipped into the lock.

Grace turned the key slowly, once, twice, *click*. She pulled the key out and placed it into her shorts' pocket, zipping it up to make sure the key was safe. As the door creaked open, she saw grass, just like a carpet, and a beautiful sapphire-blue sky. Grace crept forward, nervously. The door slammed closed, the shimmering disappeared, and so did Grace.

2

The Netherlands

On the other side, Grace no longer had her boot bag or anything else with her. Her right foot was firmly placed on top of the football and her left on the grass. Grace looked around briefly at the players who were around her. Other players were wearing orange t-shirts and orange shorts. The player in front of her smiled. Behind her new teammate she could see the towers of the Rijksmuseum and as she turned her head she could see the Johan Cruijff Arena where Ajax played.

"Kom op!"[1], the girl in front of Grace said. "We *kunnen dit!*"[2] Grace smiled, her mind still wondering what was happening, but needing to focus on the game in hand.

Over in the dugout she could see Lieke Martens hobbling with the medic. She got the attention of the player in front of her and asked what had happened to Martens.

"Lieke got injured in the warm-up, probably hamstring."

I'm in the Netherlands! Grace smiled.

The Netherlands were the current Women's European champions from the 2017 tournament. As Grace pondered this, the referee blew the whistle to start the game. Grace had no time to let this new place sink in. She recognised the player in front of her as Vivianne

---

[1] Come on
[2] We can do this!

Miedema who played for Arsenal. So, Grace passed the ball to her new friend and the game started.

Grace and the Netherlands team started with lots of possession. Grace could see the defence and the midfielders were doing well to keep the ball out of the opposition's goal by pressing and sometimes double marking. *There is good passing between the Netherlands' players*, thought Grace, and every time the Netherlands had the ball the crowd would call out the player's name–Wilms, Nouwen, Spitse, Roord– until the opposition finally got the ball from a Netherlands' player's miskick. Still, they managed to hold onto the ball, with Grace backing up when needed. *This is one way of learning the squad names.* Grace smiled to herself.

Play reached towards the opposition goalkeeper. Miedema, tried to strike the ball, but from a difficult angle the ball went across the goal. The opposition kicked the ball out for a goal kick and Grace ran off to find space towards the centre circle. The goalkeeper launched the ball high into the air and it landed on Grace's right foot.

"*Pass, pass de bal!*"[3], Grace's teammate shouted as Grace ran, dribbling the ball, into the 18-yard box.

Grace did a beautiful right-footed kick. The ball rose into the air and landed on her teammate's head. Jackie Groenen headed the ball, but sadly it went over the crossbar for the opposition to gain a goal kick. Grace ran and stopped between the centre line and the 18-yard box. The goalkeeper left-footed, kicked the ball over Grace's head and it landed in the hands of Sari Van Veenendaal, the Netherlands' goalkeeper. All the players turned and faced the goalkeeper for

---

[3] Pass, pass the ball!

another goal-kick. This gave Grace the chance to soak up the atmosphere, to try to understand what was going on, and what Sue Lopez's plan was for her.

Grace could see the sea of orange shirts waving the Netherlands flag, while some fans were singing and playing drums. As Grace turned and looked around the pitch, she could see advertising boards for the Amsterdam Tulip Museum and the Hop-on, hop-off bus tour. Grace turned and faced the goalkeeper ready for the ball to be struck hard with her right foot.

The ball took off like a rocket. This time the ball landed on the chest of an opposition player and gracefully rolled in the air down to her left foot. She tapped it ahead of her, flicked it up above her head and, with one swoop, a volley and from outside the box, the player scored an amazing goal. The ball went to the top right-hand corner and gave Van Veenendaal no chance. The Netherlands defence and midfield were awestruck, stuck like statues watching the ball come to a stop. The band stopped playing and then the whistle blew for half-time. 1–0 to the opposition.

Wow! The time flew, thought Grace. As she walked off the field she was able to take a good look at her surroundings, and felt her pocket to check the key was still there. The warm air filled Grace's lungs as she followed the rest of the Netherlands team to the coach who was standing at the dugout. The coach spoke in Dutch, so sadly Grace did not understand what was being said, but she was given lots of handshakes and pats on the back as she took sips from her red, white and blue Netherlands FA water bottle. Grace stood and turned around, arms stretched out, still in disbelief. The team, 1–0 down, had to come back in the second half.

Grace could tell that the goalkeeper and defence were told to defend and the rest had to attack; keep the ball towards the goal and keep possession. Grace knew the coach would want an early equaliser. The team became quiet, deep in thought and they could see the referee and the assistant referees ready to go again. Grace placed her hand over her back shorts' pocket (just to check she still had the key) and got ready to go back on to the pitch. Grace shook Miedema's hand as they ran gently to the centre spot to kick off again.

The fans of both teams started singing songs and cheering again as the players came back on the pitch. Both teams kept the same players on, and everyone looked fired up. The referee blew the whistle. This time Miedema started the game and, with her right foot, kicked the ball to Grace. She played it out to Danielle Van de Donk, the centre-midfielder, who right-footed the ball long to the winger. Groenen quickly ran with the ball and with her right foot kicked it into the six-yard box. By now, all players except a central defender, the goalkeeper and a couple from the opposite team were inside the 18-yard box. The central midfielder and forwards were clumped with Grace and some of the opposition players. As the ball came in, Grace tricked her marker by dodging one way and then moving the other way (something they always practised at Oaktree Fields FC) and lost the player. Seeing the ball coming towards her, she turned, and with great force, headed the ball towards the goal! The ball had a brilliant bounce, perhaps hit an uneven spot as it bounced on the ground, tricking the goalkeeper, and it went in. Grace had equalised for the Netherlands.

"Yes! Get in!" shouted Grace as the team ran to her, celebrating and hugging her.

"*Wauw! Wauw! Geweldig*!"[4] they shouted.

Now the score was back to being even: 1–1.

They quickly ran to their starting positions, waiting for the whistle and the opposition to kick off. The opposition turned up the pace and their accuracy in kicking the ball to each other. The Netherlands goalkeeper and defence worked hard to keep the ball. The minutes were running down and Grace didn't want a draw.

At last, the opposition miskicked the ball in midfield and the Netherlands team were on the counterattack. The move started again where Van de Donk pushed the ball out wide to the left-winger, Sherida Spitse. She started a

---

[4] Wow! Wow! Awesome!

run but had to kick the ball beyond herself because her marker was putting pressure on her. Just as her marker was about to go for a tackle, the winger jumped over the fallen marker and continued her run. After five steps, she looked up and saw Grace. She passed to Grace who collected the ball with her left foot and passed it to her right. Grace continued to dribble past the opposition who were motionless like trees in a forest. Grace played some very neat football. Grace made sure she was in a good position outside the box and then, with her right foot, hit the ball for goal. In slow motion, the ball flew in a straight line in the middle of the goal above the goalkeeper, who was slowly falling to the ground with her right arm stretched high. The ball went across the goalline. It landed in the back of the net, sending the Netherlands' fans in the stadium wild! Everyone jumped to their feet and cheered even louder. Grace just stood watching while her teammates ran over for the usual celebratory hugs. Grace thought it was a great time to do her little victory dance. Meanwhile, the opposition dug the ball out of the goal and ran quickly to restart. Grace ran back to her position, by which time the opposition were waiting and ready to go again. Netherlands had to keep possession. They couldn't let the opposition score in the dying minutes of the game.

Moments later the final whistle went. The score was 2–1 to the Netherlands. The Netherlands team rallied around Grace and they all hugged, shaking each other's hands in congratulation. They then showed respect to the opposing players by shaking their hands too. Her fellow centre, Vivianne Miedema, ran up to Grace.

"You did brilliantly! Well done!" she said.

Grace smiled and offered her hand to shake it. "It was a great game," Grace replied.

Grace was in awe of the fact that she had met players like Miedema who played in the Women's Super League. Everyone was gathered together, walking into the dressing room of the stadium, when Grace spotted her boot bag and water bottle. She took a large gulp of water and felt for the key in her pocket. Around her she could hear the players' excitement at winning as they all got changed ready to go home.

In a moment on her own, Grace took the key out of her pocket. Sitting down in a seat in the dugout recovering from the game, Grace stared at the key. Grace saw there was mud in between the studs of the boot and, with her fingernail, dug the mud out. The key began to shake. Sitting back in her seat, Grace took a deep breath in, holding the key tightly in her left hand, and then she disappeared.

3

Trip home

Grace found herself back at Oaktree Fields FC laying on the football pitch. People were still leaving after their training session. Grace waved at her dad. Her dad gestured at Grace to hurry up and he pointed to his watch as a sign that time was getting on and they needed to get home. Grace smiled as she walked towards her dad, knowing he had been waiting while she had been on her adventures.

"What took you so long? And you're *not* bringing another football home!" said Dad in a sarcastic tone.

"Oh, I was helping a lady to find her lost gate key," Grace replied as she got in the car, throwing her things on the floor and putting on her seatbelt. "And I can't have enough footballs to keep practising with, Dad!" Grace replied, mirroring the tone of her Dad's and giving her football a spin in her hands before placing it on the floor in front of her.

Dad started the engine and put the radio on. A lady was singing about running up a hill. Grace remembered this was the song Dad was enjoying from a series he'd been watching on WebFilms TV, and she put her shaking head in her hands in embarrassment at her dad's singing.

Finally the song was over and another song played, this time something loud and with drums. Grace tried to cut it out as she sat, staring out the open window into the midsummer evening. *Did any of that really happen? Shall I tell Beth? But what if she doesn't believe me?* Grace had questions buzzing around her mind all the way home.

"You seem very thoughtful, Grace. Everything OK?" Dad asked finally as they pulled into the drive.

"Yeah, I'm OK, just tired. It was a hard but fun training session. It's the last day of term tomorrow so it has been busy at school with sports day and making things for the school disco too," Grace answered.

She enjoyed the school year end celebrations but there was a lot to do. They got out the car and Grace watched Dad shuffle his keys around to find the front door key. This reminded Grace of her key which she could still feel in the zipped pocket of her shorts. With her mum and Benjamin not yet back from rugby, she put the water bottle and boot bag away and ran to her favourite grey chair in the living room where she lay down. Hugging her football, Grace closed her eyes.

Suddenly, she heard a loud slam of a car door and opened her eyes. Her mum and brother had returned home.

"Hi, how was football training?" Grace's mum asked.

"Yeah, it was good, hard work, but good fun!" Grace replied. "Mum, I'm quite tired. I'm going to bed".

"OK, Grace, goodnight!" Mum said as she pecked her daughter on the cheek.

"'Night, Dad!" Grace shouted.

"'Night, Grace. Well done on a really good season, you played well," Dad called as Grace ran up the stairs.

"Yeah! Well done, Grace. You did really well!" Benjamin said sarcastically.

I'll show him, Grace thought as she got ready for bed. She placed her football on the top of her chest of drawers, got under the thin sheet, took out the key from her shorts' pocket and stared at it. Moving the object around between her fingers, she thought about the football players she had met and the place she had been to. *I'll talk to Beth about it tomorrow*, thought Grace, committing herself to a chat to her best friend. With that, she placed the key under her pillow and quickly fell asleep.

"Grace, time to get up!" shouted Mum from the other side of the landing.

Grace jumped out of bed, washed, got ready for school and placed the key inside her school bag. She ran downstairs to have breakfast. It was a quiet breakfast. Everyone was tired from the evening before.

Teeth brushed and shoes on, everyone finally left the house for the last day of term.

"I'm looking forward to tonight, Mum," Grace said as she climbed into the car, "with the Euros starting in a few days' time, and it being here in England too!" Grace continued.

"Yes, it will be exciting," Mum replied.

The car arrived in the school car park. Grace got out, said her goodbyes and, with a frown at her brother, she shut the car door.

The school day was long for Grace. Her class put up decorations for the school disco and Grace enjoyed a show performed by a local theatre company. Lunchtime came, and in the playground Grace spoke to Beth.

"Football training was awesome last night," Grace started.

"Yes, it was. Are you OK, Grace?" Beth, being such a good friend, knew when Grace wasn't her usual self.

"Beth, I have to tell you something." Grace stopped, unsure whether to tell her friend, who she'd known since nursery, the truth. She decided that she would. "After football last night, a lady named Sue came up to me and gave me a key." Grace started to explain the story. Beth grinned in a *so what?* sort of way. "Beth, it was Sue Lopez, who we read about," Grace continued to explain.

"Oh yeah, Mum said there was a lady who used to play football now living somewhere here." Beth was excited about the idea of a former

England football player living in the local area.

"Well, this key she gave me is something special. It's... it's magical!" Grace looked at Beth with the most serious face she could muster, giving Beth no choice but to believe her.

"What does it do? Where is it? Show me!" Beth demanded, needing proof.

"Here, look." Grace took out the key and showed it to Beth. Beth could see it shimmer and sparkle.

"It made a door at the goalmouth appear and I went through it. Yesterday I went to the Netherlands with the Euro champions. I played football with some of the most famous women football players in the country."

Grace started to shake with nerves as she told the story. Beth sat listening to Grace, and when she finished she gave Grace a hug. Beth believed Grace as she wasn't one of those girls who made things up to make friends. She knew that Grace told her everything that happened in her life, and only her.

"Wow, Grace! This is amazing. If you ever see Lucy Bronze or Ellen White can you get their autograph for me?" Beth said to help comfort Grace. They smiled at each other.

"I'm going to the park after school to see if this key works there. You can come and see what happens if you want to, Beth." Grace invited her best friend so Beth could better understand.

"OK, meet me at mine at 4pm.". They hugged again.

"We will tell our parents that we are off to play football, just like we always do," replied Grace.

After lunch, the register was taken, then later on the end of school bell rang and the school year was over. The school disco began. Bright lights from

Disco Dom's DJ booth moved around the school hall making the glitter shimmer on the bunting the pupils had made in their art lesson earlier in the week.

Disco Dom played lots of new songs and made one of the teachers dance like a ballerina who the pupils then had to copy. Grace and Beth joined in, laughing, and when it had finished both girls complimented the teacher on their dancing.

"I'm afraid it's now the last song of the afternoon. I've had a request from some of the girls who play for Oaktree Fields FC. This one is for you!" Disco Dom shouted in his DJ voice. "It's been a great disco here at Marlbury Primary. I hope to see you all soon. Goodbye everyone!" Disco Dom finished his set and pressed 'play'. From the loudspeakers *Sweet Caroline* came on and everyone got up, waving their arms in the air and shouting the lyrics in time with the song, punching the air with clenched fists. The last part of the song finished and Disco Dom played the *Fireman Sam* theme tune as the main school hall lights came on and everyone adjusted their eyes from the darkness to the daylight. Parents and guardians began to flock into the school hall and everyone said 'bye for the summer holidays. Beth and Grace went home together with Grace's mum, singing *Sweet Caroline* as they went.

As Beth and Grace got closer to home they hugged and ran to their houses to put on their football kits. The late afternoon sun was still bright, giving the girls time to go across to the park to play.

"Off out to play football with Beth. 'Bye!" Grace called to her parents.

"Off out to play football with Grace. See ya!" Beth shouted to her parents.

Off the girls went to Prince William Park just like they always did. After a quick practice of passing the ball and a penalty shootout the girls stood together.

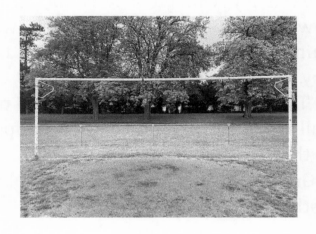

Grace took out the key from her shorts' pocket and held it in her hand. Both girls watched the key, waiting for it to do something. After what felt like ten minutes, the key began to shimmer green, white and red. Beth looked at the key in shock then at Grace then back to the key. Beth had believed Grace's story but was now seeing the shimmering for herself.

"Come here, Beth. Look at the goalmouth over there."

Grace pulled on Beth's arm, inviting her to follow her to look at the goal area. They walked across the grass towards the goalmouth which was shimmering the same colours as the key. Grace let go of Beth's arm.

"I'm going. You stay here, kick the ball around. If anyone asks, I've popped to the shop for a drink."

Grace and Beth organised the plan. Beth hugged Grace.

Grace, who was now confident about the change, put the key in, turned the key twice and ran across the threshold and landed in another football stadium.

4

Italy

Everything – the key, the goalmouth and the stadium – is green, white and red this time, thought Grace. Grace found herself walking out last behind her new teammates. She could see and hear Fara Williams and Jo Currie on the touchline speaking about Martina Piemonte being out as part of the live TV broadcast. Piemonte is out of the match because she had taken a knock in training and that the whole team had had to switch around.

Grace stood on a spot on the red carpet as she heard the start of a national anthem. Grace had heard the anthem before when watching the Italian Grand Prix as it was played every time Ferrari won a race. *Wow, I'm in Italy*! Grace beamed from ear to ear. *Maybe I'm here to help, but how will I ever get home*? Grace thought as the opposition team's anthem played. *Will I ever hear Benjamin's wind-ups and see his silly faces again*? She looked at the person next to her, who was looking straight ahead with no emotion. *Amazing*! thought Grace, suddenly feeling happier. *It's Martina Rosucci, who plays for Juventus. An amazing midfielder!* Grace smiled. Suddenly she was excited and her mind was no longer thinking about home. Grace turned to face the player again and they both smiled.

After both national anthems finished playing, the game sponsors went along the line and shook hands with each player saying, "Good luck," and, "Have a good game."

Once the last person had left, the two sets of players had their team photos taken and then ran off to their positions for kick-off. Grace ran to the centre circle waiting for a football, and as she raised her head the ball bounced down near her feet by her new teammate, Valentina Giacinti. Looking around the stadium hoardings, she could see a sign which read *Football Milan Ladies*.

"I am in Italy!" she shouted aloud this time, and the whistle was blown.

Grace remembered how Italy had won 12–0 against Israel to qualify for the European Championship in 2022.

Grace smiled as she began the game. Grace was in her usual centre-forward position. She passed the ball and looked around to find her teammates. There was no time to adjust to her surroundings; Grace had to get into the game quickly. The Italian team had all the possession and Grace ran lengths of the pitch. The football seemed quicker than the previous game, with lots of long kicks and running. Finally, the ball went out and it was the opposition's throw in. Once everyone found space, the winger threw the ball in and it was the Italian midfielder, Flaminia Simonetti, who collected it and passed it out wide to Arianna Caruso. Meanwhile, Grace was goal-side and an opposition player continued to track her. The midfield line moved forward, passing the ball amongst themselves, when eventually the ball was moving towards Grace. Grace was just inside the 18-yard box, as a lone attacker (with a marker in line with Grace). Grace took a shot on her right foot and it went in. It was a set piece goal, and the weight Grace put behind the ball made it glide through the air at speed. The ball landed at the bottom left-hand corner of the net. Grace cheered and her new Italian friends came running up to congratulate her.

"*Che grande obiettivo*"[5] and "Wow, fantastic". Rosucci gave her a hug.

Grace and friends quickly ran back to their positions, ready for the opposition team to kick off again. While Grace stood still waiting, she noticed that there was not as many fans as there had been at the Netherlands' game. She didn't understand why. Grace noticed a band playing the Italian national anthem.

The whistle blew and the opposition player passed the ball. They began their attack. 1–0 down, the opposition still looked determined to at least get a draw. Grace thought that Italy needed another goal to have a cushioned lead. The ball was passed around from player to player, along the line and back again. Grace, getting impatient with the

---

[5] What a great goal!

teasing, went in for a tackle but didn't get the ball. The referee signalled play on and the game continued. The forward took a strike at the penalty spot but the ball went wide and was deflected for a corner. *Corners are great,* thought Grace. *They give teams the chance to get in position and compose themselves.* Corners also gave Grace a chance to get her breath. The player taking the corner took a while positioning the ball exactly in the right place on the arc. The referee stood by Grace and Grace looked cheekily at her imaginary watch. The referee smiled. The whistle blew and the referee waved the player to instruct her to make a move. The player took a few steps back, held both arms in the air, and took the strike. In the box was lots of movement with players darting in and out trying not to foul the goalkeeper. The ball landed on a player's head and she headed the ball towards goal. Luckily for Grace and the Italian team, the Italian goalkeeper caught the ball. By now Grace was already towards the centre line and held her hand up in the air. The goalkeeper took no time in kicking the ball high in the air towards Grace.

Grace was free, on her own, unmarked, running with the ball towards goal, one versus one, Grace against the goalkeeper. Grace kicked the ball just as she had practiced with her Dad, and in slow motion it flew in the air, somersaulting towards the top right-hand corner. The goalkeeper had no chance. She leapt high in the air with her right hand stretched to gather the ball, but Grace's kick was too strong. The ball landed far beyond the goalline – 2–0.

Grace ran into the goal and picked up the ball and ran back to the centre circle. She placed the ball down and ran to her place while receiving pats on the back and hugs from her teammates. Grace knew she had done what she needed to do. The whistle blew and again the opposition kicked the ball to start play. Seconds later the referee blew the whistle for half-time.

The dressing rooms were neat and tidy, the walls painted white with some motivational quotes: *Sogna in grande!*[6] and, *Se ci credi, paoi farlo!*[7] Everyone enjoyed the 15 minutes because they were two–nil up. The coach's half-time speech was in Italian:

"*Continua a fare ci oche stai facendo! Goditi il gioco!*"[8]

The half-time break came to an end with the sound of a bell and the players

---

[6] Dream big!
[7] If you believe it, you can do it!
[8] Keep doing what you are doing! Enjoy the game!

started to make their way back onto the pitch. Everyone took their places. Football continued as it did in the first half – lots of long kicks and chasing. When the ball was on the ground it was hard to tackle and to get the ball. It was only through a miskick that Italy managed to get the ball again. Italy kept the ball. The ball was passed out wide and some of the players switched position while they waited for the ball to be sent into the penalty area. Grace could see the ball roll in the air towards her. She would need to time her next move to perfection. Grace jumped up high and headed the ball. The ball changed direction and moved in slow motion towards the goal. The goalkeeper was stuck between two on-side Italian players, and the ball bounced over the goalline. It came to a sudden stop. Grace stood, looking for the ball.

"Wow! A hat-trick," screamed Grace.

Giving another of her celebratory dances, this time it was accompanied by her miming a song she normally sang in front of a mirror with a hairbrush. Scoring goals could do this to players: some celebrate quietly while others do some funny things! Grace scooped the ball and kissed it. She had scored three times so she could keep the ball after the match. *Dad will be pleased with me when I bring another football home!* Grace smiled to herself.

The game started off again. The Italian team made sure they kept defending although the opposition looked defeated now. Their captain kept clapping and encouraging the team, but with few minutes left they felt the final whistle couldn't come quick enough. An Italian midfielder had the ball and was weaving in and out when a tall defender came in and mis-tackled. The defender went through the midfielder's legs and the player went flying and hit the ground with a *thump*. The referee blew the whistle to stop the game. Everyone ran over. Grace went to the player and patted her on the shoulder supportively. The referee checked on the player and waved for the physio to come on the pitch. The player looked injured. As she was receiving help, the referee brought over the player who had caused the injury and, without hesitating, went into her top pocket and pulled out a red card! The player began to walk slowly to the touchline. Meanwhile, this stoppage gave the Italian team a moment to have a drink and talk about finishing the game, while hoping their player was OK. The injured player left the pitch and decided not to carry on. Both teams played ten-a-side. The game restarted.

The Italian midfielder, Simonetti, received the ball and off they ran again to the other end of the pitch. The ball was dribbled towards the opposition goalkeeper who went in for a well-timed tackle. It rebounded off an Italian player, and the ball left the pitch for a goal-kick. The goalkeeper placed it on the corner of the six-yard box and kicked the ball with all her strength. With that, the referee's whistle blew for full-time. The Italian keeper, Giuliani, picked up the match ball and passed it to Grace.

"Well played, amazing hat-trick," the player said to Grace.

"Thanks." Grace smiled.

Grace went with her Italian teammates to the dressing room and got changed. As Grace walked towards the stadium exit, she saw that the pitch was next to the San Siro stadium where AC Milan and Inter Milan football clubs play. Afterwards, cuddling her match ball, Grace waved goodbye to her new friends and walked away.

She spent time walking around the local area. She saw many local sites such as cafes, restaurants and an ice rink. She saw a signpost for Milan cathedral close by, and she walked past one of the many parks. As Grace walked, hugging her match ball, she saw Valentina Giacinti, Aurora Galli and Martina Rosucci coming towards her.

"You were amazing today," Rosucci said.

"Thanks. You were great too. It was a team effort!" Grace replied, and then gave the ball a bounce against the concrete ground. The players left, and Grace gave one last forceful bounce of the ball before catching it and putting it under her arm. Grace took out the key and again saw it was covered in grass. Grace watched the grass fly away like a feather floating in the air as she picked it off the key. Grace then disappeared.

Grace opened her eyes slowly. She could no longer see the evening sky, which had been replaced by a daytime blue sky, and she could hear footsteps pounding towards her.

"Are you OK, Grace?" screamed Beth. "You've only been gone a minute!" continued Beth, as Grace started to slowly sit up. "Where have you been? What happened? Did you play? What was the score? Whose team were you in? Who were the opposition?" quickly asked Beth.

"OK, OK, calm down! I'll start at the beginning, if you just wait. I'm tired, and it was emotional." Grace spoke softly as she grabbed hold of Beth's hand and got to her feet. They slowly walked towards a bench and Grace began to explain what had happened.

5

Out at the park

The next day, Saturday morning, Grace woke up in bed, looking at her new ball. She bounced up and got dressed into her football kit, knowing that at 10am she would be meeting Beth to play in the park. It was quiet around the kitchen table until Mum asked:

"What is everyone doing today?"

"I'm meeting Beth at 10am. She's coming here and we're going to the park," Grace told her family.

"I'm playing games on the console and then shopping with Mum for a new rugby shirt," Benjamin said, poking his tongue out at Grace. Mum and Dad just looked at each other. Grace gave Benjamin a look that said *so what?* and shrugged her shoulders as she looked at her watch.

"Oh, I better get going, I have football to play," Grace told Benjamin, and she returned the poking-of-the-tongue gesture back at her brother. Grace raced out of the kitchen to find her trainers and put them on.

Beth jumped up onto the wall outside Grace's house and started swinging her legs, looking through her new football stickers. Grace came running out, shouting, "Got, got, got, need!" joking at Beth looking at the stickers.

"OK, Grace! I've got the Sarina Wiegman shiny!" Beth said showing off. Helped by Grace because she was giggling too much, Beth jumped off the wall while Grace held a football under her arm.

"To the park, Beth?"

"Yes, Grace. Do you have to ask?"

The girls walked to the park with Beth still looking at her stickers, and Grace linked arms with her to help guide Beth down the street.

The girls finally got to the park gate and Beth placed her stickers into her pocket to keep them safe. As always there were lots of dog walkers and runners in the park. A council gardener was watering the rose beds at one corner of the park entrance. They passed through the gate and, after walking a few yards, Grace took the ball out from under her arm. Now in both hands, she dropped the ball towards her right foot and kicked it high into the air towards the goal of the first football pitch. Both girls ran together to chase the ball. The girls looked at each other.

"Last one there goes in goal!" the girls both shouted together.

This was the game they always played and they took it in turns being in goal. Grace was last at the goal because today something caught her eye and stopped her in her tracks. On the bench, sat a girl with her face in her hands looking sad.

"Shall we go and say hi?' Beth asked.

"Yes, let's. It's not nice seeing someone sad. I wonder what's wrong." With a concerned look on their faces, both girls ran over to the bench. As the girl saw them coming over, she started to lift her head away from her hands and sat up.

"Hi, are you OK?" Grace asked.

"No, not really," the girl replied.

"Why not?" Beth asked.

"I'm sad seeing you play football together. I want to play football but the places my mum has rung have said you have to have trials. I just want to play; I don't know if I'm any good. I just want to make new friends and play!" The girl began to get upset.

"You could always join our club," Grace said, sitting next to the girl on the bench.

"Thanks. I see you both playing a lot and hoped I would see you today," the girl continued.

"You don't need a trial at our club, everyone is welcome. We get shown skills, and we play together." Grace spoke to the girl calmly, trying to reassure her.

"That sounds really good." The girl looked up, wiping the tears from her eyes. "Where do you play?"

"At Oaktree," Beth came in, smiling, now sitting the other side of the girl.

"Oh no, it's too far away. My mum doesn't drive and it's two bus rides away. We've already talked about Oaktree!" sobbed the girl.

"Where do you live?" Grace asked.

"In those flats over there." Wiping tears away, the girl pointed in the direction of the tall building poking through the oak trees.

"My name is Grace. I could talk to my parents about maybe taking you as you only live around the corner from me."

"Yeah!" jumped in Beth, "I'm sure they will be able to take you. Get your mum to call Sam our coach to get a space! And I'm Beth, by the way." Beth put out her hand to greet her new friend. The girl then held out both her hands for Grace and Beth to shake one each.

"I'm Lottie. I've just moved here to be closer to my grandma. She isn't well at the moment."

"Do you want to play football with us now?" Grace asked.

"I'll be in goal," Grace shouted, as the three ran towards the goal. Beth and Lottie took it in turns to shoot penalties and then free kicks and then swapped over so everyone had a turn in goal.

The girls began by passing the ball in a triangle so they could talk.

"What school do you go to?" Grace asked after a short time of kicking the ball around.

"I'm starting Marlbury Primary in September. I'll be in year 6," Lottie replied now happier, smiling and laughing with her new friends. "I've been here a few weeks, but I couldn't start school until the new term," Lottie finished.

"That's great, you'll be in the same year as us!" Beth was excited, bouncing up and down.

The trio changed their game to penalty practice.

"I'll go in goal," Beth volunteered, and Grace and Lottie took it in turns to shoot. Lottie took the ball in her right foot and dribbled it onto the penalty spot. She took two steps back and went for a short run up. Lottie struck the ball hard with her right foot. The ball flew in the air towards the top left-hand corner of the goalmouth. Beth jumped high to try to stop the ball but it flew past her hands and out the other side of the goalline.

"Wow, what a goal!" Grace shouted, running towards Lottie to celebrate. Beth couldn't hear them celebrating as she had gone running after the ball which had now trickled all the way to the next football pitch.

Clutching the ball, Beth ran to the other girls and congratulated Lottie on a superb penalty. "You really need to join our team!"

"I'll go in goal now!" Lottie ran towards the goalmouth and Beth placed the ball onto the penalty spot. Taking 10 steps backwards, she put her hands on her hips thinking about where she was going to place the ball. With a deep breath in, Beth took a run up. She put far too much foot under the ball which made it go high into the air and it landed in between Beth and Lottie in goal.

"Whoops," screamed Beth, as Lottie ran towards the ball to catch it with both hands.

"I think it's time for a break," Beth sighed. "I've got enough money for all three of us to get a drink from the hut."

The girls talked football while Lottie carried the ball, smiling at her new friends.

"What football team do you both support?" Lottie asked.

Grace and Beth smiled at each other, and Grace took it upon herself to answer Lottie's question:

"We both watch lots of the Women's Super League and the Lionesses."

Lottie agreed that she watched lots too. "It is really good that they are showing more on TV now!" Lottie said.

"We sometimes go with my dad to watch Oaktree Fields too. My dad sometimes volunteers to man the turnstiles and tea hut," Grace said. As the girls were getting closer to the hut they decided what drink they wanted.

"Morning, girls. What would you all like today?" the man at the hut asked.

Beth said, "Hi. Please can we have three strawberry smoothies? Thanks."

"Coming right up. So, have you scored many goals so far this morning?"

"Not many, we've been practising our penalties," Grace said as she took two of the drinks and passed one to Lottie.

"That's £6 then, please. Thank you," the man said.

"Thank you," chorused the three girls.

"I'm sure I'll see you again tomorrow," he said.

"Yep, see you tomorrow!" Beth called back.

With their drinks, they walked around the whole park talking about school and the football club.

"It's time I went home. Thanks for the drink and for letting me play in your game," Lottie said after swallowing the last of her drink.

"Can I take your phone number so I can ask if you are free to play football?" Grace stood waiting with her phone to take her number. "Make sure you get your mum to ring Sam," Grace said. "And we will speak to our parents. I hope you can come with us, you will have fun!"

Back at the pitch, Beth and Grace could see Lottie leaving the park through the gate and she closed it gently behind her. As the girls stood watching, Beth stated, "I better go home too. It's been a good morning of playing!"

"Yes, I'll see you tomorrow. And let's make sure we say something to our parents because everyone should be able to play football. How do any of us know we are any good unless we have a go?" Grace stated as she took out the key from her pocket.

"Yep, see you tomorrow!" Beth shouted as she started running towards the gate.

Grace stared at the key she had taken from her shorts' pocket. The key began to glow gold, red and black. Grace looked around and saw that other people in the park were either leaving or going in the opposite direction to Grace. In the nearest goal, Grace could see the same colours shining through, turning into what looked like the Reichstag building with all its large windows and pillars. Grace didn't waste any time. She got up and ran across to the goal. Turning the key in the lock twice, she was over the goalline and into another stadium.

6

Germany

This time Grace understood the language because she had learned a lot at home from her mum and was learning German in school too.

Again, her right foot rested on the sphere and Grace looked around, trying to figure out which German town she was in. There came news that Lea Schuller was ill in the dressing room and couldn't play. Grace was sad for her but knew it was a good chance for her. At least Schuller could rest this game and be ready for the next international game in a few days' time.

The whistle blew for kick off and Grace passed the ball to Svenja Huth, her new centre-forward friend who was dressed in a white t-shirt and black shorts with a trim in the same colours as the German flag. The game began. The game started well for Grace and the German team. The defender, Giulia Gwinn, kicked the ball to the winger, Lena Oberdorf, and like the wind she ran all the way down the right wing, using the fullness of the pitch. The player crossed the ball to where Grace stood, and as she had always managed to do, she headed the ball with power. The ball hit the back of the net, almost burning a hole through it. Germany was one up. Was it too early to score? This could give the opposition lots of time to catch up.

"Was fur ein tolles ziel!"[9] was chanted by the crowd and her teammates.

---

[9] What a great goal!

The opposition had other feelings; looks of scowling and frowns that could be seen as sore losing. Grace smiled and she ran back to her position ready to set off again. This time things became difficult for Grace. The opposition had the ball and passed it among themselves, trying to gain some pace. Finally, the German midfielder, Sara Dabritz, tackled a player and managed to get the ball away which then landed at Grace's feet. Grace had turned the ball, ready to start attacking, when an opposition player returned the tackle. Instead of touching and connecting with the ball, the player found Grace's ankle. Grace fell to the ground clutching her right ankle – the one that scored goals and magically dribbled the ball around the opposition.

"Not my goal-scoring foot!" screamed Grace. Grace was in agony. The pain was worse than the time she fell off her bike and hurt her arm. The team's first aider ran onto the pitch and the game was stopped for the injury. *I wonder if the key will help my ankle?* Grace wondered as she lay her head down on the ground, clutching her ankle. Grace's ankle was attended to by the first aider with sprays and massages while Grace found the magic key and gently rubbed it.

The power of both healed Grace's pain, and the first aider and a teammate helped her up. Meanwhile, the opposition player was given a yellow card. The referee looked at her watch and worked out the number of extra minutes that needed to be added at the end of the first half.

The game continued. Germany were awarded a free kick, which was taken quickly, and it landed at the other end of the pitch, collected by the goalkeeper. The opposition goalkeeper kicked the ball with power and it ended up at the foot of one of the centre-forwards. With some smart dribbling around the German goalkeeper, Merle Frohms, the opposition scored in the empty net.

'*How embarrassing would that have been if she missed the empty net?*' thought Grace as she slowly walked back to the centre spot to kick off. *Surely it's nearly the end of the first half.* Grace was sure it was and as she waited and watched, the referee blew the whistle to restart. Grace passed the ball to Huth and, with that, the referee whistled for half-time.

Grace ran to collect her water bottle and listened to the coach's half-time chat. *This game is tough because the team haven't won their last three games and are now fearing they won't reach the European Championships. It won't ever be a good tournament without them there!* Grace pondered this while she ate a half-time snack.

After 10 minutes everyone ran back onto the pitch. It was the other team's turn to kick off.

"Komm schon!"[10] the German captain shouted and clapped to gee up her team.

Grace heard the crowd continue their chanting and the playing of drums to help motivate the team. The second half began; the German team continuing in the traditional four-four-two formation. The opposition took the kick off. The central midfielder, Lina Magull, collected the ball and passed it out wide to the wing, but the ball was passed back to the opponent, who high-kicked it towards Grace. She missed the header because the ball flew a foot above her head. The ball was caught by the goalkeeper. The goalkeeper rolled the ball out to the right-back who kicked the ball to the central defender. She then kicked the ball

---

[10] Come on!

long and wide for other players to chase, but it landed outside the line, giving the Germans a throw. The German winger, Oberdorf, threw the ball overhead to the midfield who saw Grace and her partner-in-crime, Huth, up front running towards goal. She kicked the ball to Grace who ran, dribbling the ball towards goal. She passed the ball, and her fellow forward scored. It was as if the forward was going to tap it low, kidding the goalie, but then the ball went into the right-hand side of the goal, leaving the goalkeeper to pick herself up off the floor and scoop the ball out from the net.

"Gut gemacht! Du bist ein grossartiger spieler,"[11] said Oberdorf to Grace. Grace had helped her score by reading the game correctly. She'd got into a good

---

[11] Well done! You're a great player!

position and that had helped give the player passing the ball options.

The team were beaming as they were now 2–1 up. Grace knew her being there helped the team spirit. The German team could see the opposition increasing the pressure. This game meant a lot to Germany. It would mean they would qualify to compete in the tournament in England. The opposition created lots of chances; quick passing and headers between players. However, Germany played best when the ball was on the ground. The opposition central defender had the ball and slowly pushed everyone forward. She kicked the ball into the 18-yard box where it bounced into the six-yard box and the forward headed it over the crossbar for a goal-kick. The goal-kick sadly landed on the head of the opposition midfielder who ran with the ball and passed it out to the winger. She then crossed the ball into the goal area. By now, the number four, the tallest girl in the opposing team, was in the goal area and she headed the ball. The ball went to the top of the net, crossing the line. Goal! It was now 2–2.

Germany still wanted to win, but the team began to panic with only 10 minutes remaining. The want to score the winning goal was shown on all the players' faces.

Grace kicked off. She passed the ball to a central midfield player and started to make a run for it towards goal. This time the German team kept possession of the ball, kicking the ball between players, playing head tennis and then getting the ball on the ground, showing off their dribbling skills. Oberdorf, the German winger, started a long run towards goal – the start of the attack. However, an opposition player took a chance and went in for a well-timed tackle resulting in a throw-in for Germany. Oberdorf got up off the ground and picked up the ball. She took three steps forwards and threw the ball overhead. *Why didn't the referee move her back along the line?* thought Grace, smiling. By now she was quite close to the corner flag as Oberdorf threw the ball back on.

Collected by Grace, she passed the ball to the thrower who was moving again to find space. The wing had to kick the ball hard over players towards goal. However, this time the ball was easily collected by the opposite number one. The goalkeeper miskicked the ball out of the area and it was collected by Grace who, with her first touch, kicked the ball hard. It stayed in the air and, slowly rotating, it started to sparkle with the colours of the German flag as it flew across the air, now hovering above the goalkeeper as it crossed the goalline. 3 –2. *This has to be game over now!* thought Grace.

The opposition got back to their positions and the game quickly restarted. They were fired up! Grace ran everywhere, trying to score or assist chances, and also defend their 3–2 lead. Grace took time with the ball, looking around to see whom she could give it to. However, in doing that, the opposite midfielder came in for the ball and was instantly on the counterattack. The opposing team passed the ball neatly. Their winger chipped the ball in and their striker got a head to the ball. Goal! 3–3. *How did that happen?* pondered Grace. *We've fallen asleep and got complacent – as Sam calls it – thinking we've won! The game isn't over yet!* Grace frowned.

At last, the ball made its way back to the centre point with Grace who stood there and shouted, "Aufleuchten! Nicht einschlafen! Das dürfen wir jetzt nicht verlieren!"[12]

Everyone looked at Grace as the referee blew the whistle to restart. Grace passed the ball to Huth, who passed to Oberdorf, and the German team started a rally of good passing with the crowd chanting every time a German player touched the ball. Grace just watched the ball go to every player until someone broke for an attack, but it didn't happen.

The ball made its way to the German keeper, Fromhs, who kicked the ball as far up field as she could. This reached Huth who, with her usual tricks, attempted to get the ball towards the goal.

With that, the shrill sound of the final whistle was heard. 3–3 *What a relief*, thought Grace with a deep sigh.

---

[12] Come on! Don't fall asleep! We can't lose this now!

It was now a penalty shoot-out to decide who would win.

The teams huddled together with their respective coaches, and the players on the bench handed out the drinks and words of encouragement. While the players had a drink, some started to volunteer to be penalty takers, and so the team managers finalised names. The referee blew the whistle to get the finale under way. All Grace could do was watch nervously.

The captains went to the referee who tossed a coin to see whose goal they would use and which team would start. Grace watched as the referee pointed to the goal where the German supporters were. The opposition would start first. Both teams got ready and the referee placed the match ball onto the penalty spot. Grace started pacing up and down, feeling even more nervous.

Each team had taken three penalties, and it was the turn again of a German player. The ball was on the penalty spot and the player took three steps back, did a few quick runs on the spot, and charged up to the ball, kicking it with all her might towards goal making it 4–3 to Germany. *Oh, this is so tense!* Grace thought, still pacing around the pitch between the German players. The opposite striker who had scored the goal in the match to make it even, stepped up. Taking her time, she placed the ball on the spot and started staring at the goalkeeper. *And here come the mind games*, thought Grace as she covered her face with her hands and peeped between her fingers. The striker danced on the spot, took four steps back and stopped, bracing herself for the run up! Off she ran, her toes catching the bottom of the ball, sending it flying over the goalkeeper and over the crossbar.

"Wow, what a shot! You need to join my brother's rugby team!" Grace laughed.

But Grace soon stopped when reality hit. The German team looked at Grace and passed her the ball. Grace was the fifth person in the German team to take a penalty. Grace walked calmly to the spot, clenching the ball between both hands. She kissed the ball and put it on the spot. Grace looked at the goalkeeper and to the left, then she looked to the right. *This will trick the goalkeeper – she won't know where I'm going to put it,* thought Grace. Grace took two steps back and went for the run up. Her foot was positioned perfectly on the ball and it chipped over the goalkeeper and into the back of the net. This sent Grace running around the pitch towards the German team, the crowd on their feet, cheering and waving flags.

Everyone ran to Grace and they began to take her arms and legs to give

Grace the bumps. Up and down, Grace was moved into the air. She started to feel sick and the German team put her down gently. With hugs and celebrations for achieving enough to go to England, they packed up their things and went off to celebrate at the Augustiner am Gendarmenmarkt for the best sausages in Berlin.

The football supporters left the stadium, Grace was alone and it became quiet. It was very late at night; past Grace's bedtime by the time the game had finished. There was no time for Grace to join the team celebrating in Berlin, but Grace had already seen the Germans' passion for football. Grace sat in the dugout and she thought about all the teams she had played alongside. She didn't care who she was playing against for she simply enjoyed playing. She enjoyed being part of a team and helping that team to achieve. The games she played brought people together; football brings people together.

Grace went to the pocket of her shorts and pulled out the key. Grace found blades of grass and picked these off the key. Rubbing the key, Grace felt a strange sensation. *I've got that feeling mum says is like butterflies and feeling tired*, thought Grace.

Grace fell asleep, dreaming about the penalty shoot-out, and then she disappeared.

7

Stadium away-day

It was Sunday morning, and because of the Saturday afternoon game Grace woke up later than normal. Grace rubbed her eyes, still feeling tired from playing and the excitement of the penalty shoot-out. Grace lay in bed smiling about scoring that final penalty, going through it again in her mind. Her thoughts came back to her room and lying in bed. From a distance, she could hear her mum talking to someone on the phone.

News came through to Grace and Beth that Lottie had a place at Oaktree Fields FC next season.

"Grace, it's great news that Lottie can play with you and Beth at Oaktree next season!" Dad called to her.

"It is, Dad. I knew Sam would be inclusive. There will be a few new coaches too," Grace stated.

"Well, how about we do some Oaktree team bonding and I'll take the three of you on a stadium tour? Somewhere special" Dad suggested.

"Yeah, what a great idea! I'll ring Beth and Lottie and see if they are free soon."

Dad switched on his mobile phone to order the tickets.

Some while later, Dad, Grace and Beth got into the car and took a five-minute journey to collect Lottie. Grace and Beth got out the car and pressed the buzzer for Lottie's flat. Her mum answered.

"She's already on her way down!" shouted Lottie's mum through the speaker.

"OK, thanks!" Grace and Beth sang in chorus, waiting for Lottie to appear. It was a long drive to the large city close to where they live in Marlbury. Dad decided it would be a great idea to play all the old football songs to get everyone in the mood for the trip.

As they walked along the path towards the entrance door, they could see a statue of the previous manager, and the club shop.

"We will leave the shopping until we are about to leave," Dad said. They continued walking around the stadium, looking above at the photos of some of the current football players who play for the team beaming down at them. The four got to the tour door and Dad showed the tickets on his phone to the scanner and they went through the turnstiles.

"Morning. The next tour is in 10 minutes, so feel free to look round the trophy cabinet," a man dressed in a yellow hi-vis jacket said. The girls walked over to the latest silverware the team had won, where a man dressed in a black suit with white gloves looked after a trophy.

"It must be a real trophy," Beth whispered to Grace and Lottie.

"You can have your photo taken with the trophy, if you want to," said the man who was watching over the trophy.

Grace's dad loaded the camera app on his phone and took a photo of the girls with the trophy, and then a photo of them each, one at a time.

"I'll e-mail these photos to your parents in a while," dad said to Beth and Lottie.

"Good morning. Yes, it's still morning!" As the man shouted to get everyone's attention, he looked jokingly at his watch. "Good morning and welcome to this amazing stadium. You have all seen our trophy cabinet and our new sparkling addition! It is from the latest win in the Marlbury Choc Cup. We are so proud of the team for coming back from a 2–0 setback at half-time to win 4–2." The tour guide smiled and looking at the trophy, proud of the team's achievements. "So, let's go on the tour.

"On this tour you will see the history of the club – when times were challenging and also those good times." The tour guide gave the trophy a quick tap as he walked passed, and everyone followed him.

"Lottie," Grace whispered to get her attention, "Marlbury has a brilliant chocolate factory on the industrial estate. We will have to show you." They followed the tour guide through the archway to the exhibition.

"That would be great!" Lottie replied.

"So, as I said in my introduction, the start of the club was challenging during World War Two, but we had a wonderful women's team playing to help keep everything going. We are very proud of its history and continue to have a thriving women's team and youth academy today." The tour guide smiled towards the three girls. "Please look at the memorabilia from previous players and donations made by fans. I can only give you 15 minutes though because there is a lot here to see. Then we will move to the team dressing room and the media station." The tour guide moved away and started chatting to the security lady. Grace and her friends walked quickly towards the old football shirts and they read out the names of the players they could see.

"Look, you two, it's Rachel Brown-Finnis's goalkeeper's shirt!" Grace shouted, pointing at the shirt.

"Wow! Look at her goalkeepers' gloves. They look a bit big!" Lottie said as she lifted a hand and compared hers to the gloves.

"I think I might have some growing to do," Lottie thought aloud, with a sad look on her face.

"If you want to be a goalkeeper, be a goalkeeper, Lottie," Grace's dad said to Lottie. "I always tell Grace, if you want to do something then give it a go. You don't know unless you try." Grace's dad smiled as the girls listened to his words.

They all smiled. The sun suddenly shone through the window and this made the Estimate FM-sponsored shield sparkle.

"Right, everyone!" The tour guide got everyone together. "We will now move on to the team dressing rooms." Everyone followed the leader, and the large door open on the other side was colourful and bright.

On the walls were messages to help the home team's players get motivated for the game. Ahead of the group was a door that had a referee sign on it, and further along the corridor was a red door that read: *home team*.

"So, everyone, here is where the team get changed. You see that TV? They will watch games and see replays to think about how they can change their game so they can play better, or to see how they can keep playing well to help them win again." The tour guide smiled as he spotted the three girls finding the players' names and sitting on their seats. The seating area was in a semi-circle so everyone could see everyone else. A table stood in the middle with bottles of water on it. It was a stage for the manager and staff to give the team talks.

Soon afterwards, the tour guide gathered the visitors and they began to walk towards the pitch. There was tape across the dugouts asking people to keep off the grass. The whole group walked around in a circle, taking in the size of the stadium and the pitch. "Wow!" everyone said together as they took the place in.

"The last part of the tour is the media station. Come, follow me." Off went the tour guide and the herd followed him back inside and along the corridor. Inside the media station were offices where journalists from the newspapers and TV sat and re-watched parts of the game to write reports, and sponsor stands were on the walls where the media interviewed the players. Grace found the press area where managers and players sat to be interviewed by the media. She grabbed Beth and Lottie by the hands and told them to sit behind the desk.

"Lottie, you can be Sarina and Beth, you're Leah! I'm Alex Scott and I'll interview you," Grace told the girls, and the three acted out the scene.

"Hi, you have just won the Euros, how do you feel?" Grace began, making her right hand into a fist and pretending it was a microphone.

"Well, it was a great game. We performed our best and we got the job done," Lottie said smiling, as the group began to look on at the girls.

"Yes, we defended well and we had great play which created the best goals. It was really an amazing team performance," Beth finished.

With that, the tour guide cheered and the group joined in. "You are naturals. One day you may do this with real cameras rolling." The tour guide smiled. "Well, with that post-match interview comes the end of our tour. I hope you have enjoyed it. We will now go to the club shop where I'll bid you all farewell." The tour guide led everyone to the club shop. Everyone said goodbye and thanked the tour guide and he said the same to the visitors. The tour guide high-fived the girls and said, "We hope to see you three back here as players." The girls smiled and looked at each other, nodding.

Inside the club shop Lottie spotted a pair of goalkeepers' gloves and put them on. Grace and Beth looked at the t-shirts and smiled at Grace's dad to purchase the lot, so Dad did! Lottie wore the goalkeepers' gloves all the way home in the car.

Dad dropped the girls off at the park so Lottie could try out her new gloves. Grace took the football out of the car boot and they walked to the gate.

With Lottie in goal and Grace and Beth outfield in the penalty area, they talked about the football shirts and the silverware they had seen at the stadium.

"Pretending to be Leah Williamson in the media station was amazing!" exclaimed Beth as she took a shot towards goal. The ball went through the goal and out the other side. It was stopped by Sue Lopez who was out walking her dog with another lady.

"Grandma!" Lottie shouted.

"Your grandmother is with Sue? We must tell them what we saw today," Grace said with great excitement.

"Sue is my grandma's neighbour," Lottie continued, speeding up her walking. "They always talk about football over the fence or they go to each other's house for tea and a chat. They are so pleased we are all friends".

The girls told the two women all about their day.

"I'm going back to my flat with Grandma now because she might need my help to get home to my mum's.

"Anyway, I'm going now. Thanks for a lovely day. I'll see you both tomorrow. Or Tuesday," said Lottie cheerfully. They all hugged. Beth and Grace went to the bench near the pitch and watched as Lottie, her grandma and Sue left through the gate.

"I'm getting tired too!" Beth yawned. "I'll see you tomorrow." Beth hugged Grace and she too walked out the gate of Prince William Park.

Grace sat alone. She took out the key and thought about her day trip with her friends and everything she had seen at the stadium. Clutching the key, it began to sparkle green and white in shape of the Giant's Causeway. Grace's attention now went to the nearest goal, and with a new level of energy, she bounced up and ran to the goal. "It's turning green and white," she smiled.

A green, pentagon-shaped door appeared. Turning the key once then twice the door unlocked and Grace walked through. "Football *is* for everyone," Grace shouted as she passed the white goalline.

8

Northern Ireland

Grace walked through the goal and appeared in a changing room. There was lots of chatter about work (full-time jobs not football work!) Grace, until now, had only visited international teams who played professionally. Grace sat and listened to the discussions:

"Some women's international teams have been professional for a long time; some not very long," one of the Northern Ireland team players stated.

"Maybe things will change for us," replied her team member.

Looking around, Grace noticed that this team were all in green with white socks, and looking at the crest on their shirts saw they represented Northern Ireland but were semi-professional. One of the players, Lauren Wade, who works for her family business had sadly been called back home; another player was not able to play because she was a nurse (they were short-staffed and she was on the night shift).

The coach saw Grace and pointed at the position number nine in the changing room. She got changed. Grace could hear the chatter change to the game in hand, and tactics made the game sound serious.

"OK, let's enjoy this game!" shouted Marissa Callaghan, the Northern Ireland captain.

"We can do this," everyone shouted in chorus.

"Their number seven is looking for the tournament golden boot and the passing from the wings have been outstanding, so we need to narrow them down," Callaghan continued.

The Northern Ireland manager began his team talk and the team sat listening. Grace thought about the part she would be playing in this game.

The team started to line up outside the dressing room, ready to walk towards the pitch. The stands and seats were red at this stadium, with banners of the Women's Euros. The referee and the two assistants started to walk through the tunnel and onto the pitch, and the teams followed. The teams stood in the long line and in front of them was a long line of children from local schools. Everyone waited for the national anthem. Grace knew that this time the anthem would only play once.

After *God Save the King* rang out, Grace followed the players in front and fist-pumped the opposition in the line. Grace took off her green training top and gave it to the kit man. She ran to her position as forward to kick off the match.

Grace could see the referee waiting with her two assistants for the two captains. Once they arrived, they shook hands with one another and swapped national crests to mark the occasion. The referee tossed the coin to find out which end the teams would be attacking. *Why don't they just have a game of 'rock, paper, scissors' in the dressing room?* Grace thought.

Everyone took their seats or positions, and the referee checked that the players and Grace were ready to get the game going. The whistle shrilled and off Grace went. She passed the ball to Callaghan and it quickly went to the opposition for a throw in. The opposition were dressed in white shirts, white shorts and red socks. This time the players' names were on the back of shirts so she could see who she was playing with and against. The ball came off an opposition player across the touchline and it was a Northern Ireland throw. Grace took the ball from the throw on her head and controlled it onto her right foot. She then kicked the ball long.

The ball was too long for Laura Rafferty, and the opposition goalkeeper caught it and threw it to the left-back. The opposition had a lot of possession by passing along the defence line and then introducing someone from midfield, just to make it interesting. The opposition number two had the ball and started at speed to run the length of the pitch. Grace could see her teammate Kirsty McGuiness put pressure on the right-back and went in for a tackle. The tackle was late. McGuiness caught the player, who went down, and the opposition were awarded a free-kick.

Grace was watching on. The free-kick was taken quickly and the opposition continued their passing; this time along the midfield line, now and again in triangles and also now and again introducing a defender into the kick-about. The opposition then picked up the pace and the central-defender kicked the ball long to their forward. With a header, it was punched away by Jackie Burns, the Northern Ireland goalkeeper.

Rafferty cleared the ball away and everyone ran towards the Northern Ireland attack; again, picked up by the opposition and again passed in triangles and along the line of defence. Grace thought that her team were finding it a challenge to get away.

All of a sudden in the box, the referee whistle blew for hand ball against the Northern Ireland team. Grace thought the ball came off Rafferty's upper arm but her arms were close to her body. Here came the slowest four minutes for Grace while it was checked with VAR (Video Assistant Referee). Grace kept warm by darting in and out of the opposition and making glasses with both her thumbs and forefingers, dancing around Ellen White!

The whistle blew and the free-kick was awarded to Northern Ireland for an earlier hand-ball. *This has given us a lifeline,* Grace thought. *Far better result than a penalty so soon in the game!* Burns took the free-kick and it travelled all the way down to the other end to then be kicked all the way back.

Grace tried her best to chase after the ball but the opposition midfield were far too quick. They passed the ball to a midfield player who was on a tight angle and the ball was saved by the goalkeeper's left foot. Grace went up to her and tapped her on the shoulder. "Great save!" Grace shouted. So, the game continued; more passing made by the opposition, and still Northern Ireland found them a difficult team to break down.

Grace chased the opposition midfield with the ball and took it and passed the ball to Rafferty, who was so close to the goalkeeper she attempted, to shoot but the ball was picked up by the opposition's goalkeeper. The goalkeeper kicked to her defence and off they went. Grace was getting tired and frustrated now with all the running, chasing long balls and trying to defend some strong passing and shooting. Grace and the Northern Ireland team kept being resilient but it became too much.

The opposition's first goal came from a right foot over the goalkeeper into the top right-hand corner. The game restarted. The second came from a corner and was defended by Furness and then McGuiness but found their midfielder again and, with a little deflection, went along the ground on the left-hand side. Grace watched as the ball trickled along the ground. After what felt like minutes, the ball eventually stopped across the goalline. Grace picked up the ball and skipped to the centre circle spot and restarted the game. Finally, the whistle blew for half-time.

It was 2–0 to the opposition.

Grace walked to the tunnel with Rafferty, talking about her football and how her team, Southampton, had been promoted to the championship. They talked about Sue Lopez.

"Yes, she is our greatest fan. She often comes and watches us," Rafferty stated.

During half-time there were lots of drinks and snacks eaten to build up the energy for the second half. The coach talked about keeping the pressure on and enjoying the game. Grace looked around, and although until now didn't know much about the Northern Ireland team, she felt a sense of pride for them; a team of players who had full-time jobs and still achieved a seat at the Euros table. Everyone left the dressing room fired up, knowing their target was to keep marking players and work towards breaking the opposition down and maybe, just maybe, break the oppositions' clean sheet record.

The opposition had many substitutions at half-time and with these fresh legs continued the second half as they finished the first – lots of passing, along the lines and in triangles. Grace just stood watching! The opposition had another break in pace, and quickly after the start of the second half they scored their third goal. Grace watched as the ball was crossed from the wide midfield player and into the six-yard box. 3–0 by a neat volley. Grace looked around, waiting for everyone to be ready, and she started the game again. Grace found a little spark to keep the Northern Ireland team focused and lift the spirits of a team who had begun to run with lowered heads.

Grace had the ball and with some beautiful footwork she began a break. She passed the ball to Furness who gave it back. Grace passed the ball, heading for Rafferty, but the ball was taken again and away the opposition went. Grace turned and started to chase after the opposition players but all she could do was run. The fans around the stadium were singing and banging drums. She looked at the Northern Ireland fans who were still singing and waving their flags. The opposition's fourth goal came from another energetic break. The forward took it and this time the ball, with great speed, went right and into the goal. The goalkeeper went in the right direction but just couldn't get a hand to it, and the speed of it going in was hard to defend. Grace was laying on the ground next to the goalscorer, her head looking towards goal to check where it went.

"You must've burnt a hole in the net with a strike at that speed," Grace complimented the goalscorer next to her.

The player just smiled, got up, and started celebrating the goal with her teammates and fans. By now the ringing of football songs was heard all over Southampton (except for the little pocket of loyal Irish fans in the corner). *Surely that was game over*, Grace thought, trying her best to console the Irish players who were more deflated than ever.

"You must keep positive," shouted Grace. "Keep playing well, keep pressing! It may not feel like it now, but this game is the first game for the Northern Ireland women's football of the future! You are trailblazers!" continued Grace.

This is why Grace's dad thought she would make a good captain–she always said the right thing–and the Northern Ireland squad gathered round to restart the game with heads held high knowing this game was the start of their future.

But the game went from bad to worse. Goal five came at the hands of an own goal. Grace ran down towards the opposition's goal and, from a lovely cross, Grace got on the end of it and accidently chipped the ball over the Northern Ireland goalkeeper and into the back of the net. The goalkeeper tried to jump to get a hand to it but the ball went too high. Grace turned, putting her head in her hands. Grace turned to the referee to ask how long was left of the game.

"Seconds!" replied the referee, and Grace gave a sigh of relief.

The Irish players were sad; some crying and some comforted by the opposition. However, the Northern Ireland team had made their mark in a major tournament. Grace shook hands with the opposition and then started to make a chain with the Northern Ireland team. They began to run towards the fans and saluted them by bowing together, thanking them for attending and being loyal during this match and the whole tournament.

Meanwhile, on the other side of the pitch, there was lots to celebrate, players and fans singing *Sweet Caroline* and *Football's coming home*, and dancing. The opposition were on their way to the quarter-finals.

The Northern Ireland players began to walk towards the tunnel, and Grace sat on the pitch listening and watching the opposition singing and dancing with their fans. Grace unzipped the pocket in her shorts and took out the key. She saw a blade of long grass and some mud all over the key. Grace lay on the pitch and looked up into the late evening sky. A tear trickled down her face, which was removed by the slight wind coming off the Solent. They were a mixture of happy and sad tears; sad because the team she played for had lost, but happy that this game gave Northern Ireland women's football a voice. Grace rubbed the mud off the key and started to feel prouder. *And people say this is just a game*, whispered Grace, and with that Grace disappeared.

9

Planning the adventure with Beth

Grace awoke, laying on her bed with the key held in her hand. It was still dark. She looked at her watch: 10.20pm. *How long have I been asleep?* she wondered. She took her mobile phone and started to text Beth:

> I've been on my adventures again! Meet me at 10am at the park.

Grace placed the key under her pillow and fell back to sleep.
Beth okayed Grace's idea.

The next morning as arranged, Grace and Beth met at the pitch. They gave each other a hug and sat on the ground leaning against the bottom of one of the goal posts. Grace began to explain her adventure:

"I was in Southampton and I played for the Northern Ireland team. They are semi-professional, and the game was during a tournament. They lost and I scored an own goal." Grace's head lowered. "I didn't mean to. The ball just ended on my feet and bounced the wrong way," continued Grace.

"Oh, Grace! These things happen," Beth said sympathetically. Beth knew what it was like to score own goals.

"The crowd were great, and the Northern Ireland team had a small crowd of loyal fans. It was great. They are so proud!" Grace stopped and looked at Beth. "I want to see if you can come with me next time," suggested

Grace. "I want you to experience the game like I have – the fans, the players, the drums and the songs!" concluded Grace. "It's magic! Football *is* coming home." Grace hugged Beth, and they walked towards home. Grace and Beth organised their plan and said goodbye.

Grace spent the day watching TV and thinking about what her next adventure would be like with Beth. As night fell, Grace lay on the grey sofa and changed the TV channel to watch football. It was the start of the opening ceremony at Old Trafford for the Women's Euros tournament. There were lots of fireworks and smoke. "How can the Lionesses see where they are going?" Grace said aloud, concerned that the smoke wouldn't disperse by the time kick off came.

Grace checked her trusted pocket for the key: it was still there. With a smile, feeling tired Grace's heavy eyelids closed. She fell asleep.

The next morning, Grace found herself in bed still wearing her football kit. Mum knocked, opened the door and walked over the threshold. "You must've worn yourself out at the stadium, and playing football with your friends this week! You missed the whole England game," Mum stated as Grace rubbed her eyes. "Come on, sleepy head, breakfast is ready downstairs. We have your favourite: hash browns, sausages and baked beans."

Mum always knew how to say the right thing because with that, Grace jumped out of bed and got ready for the day, putting on a clean t-shirt, shorts and football socks. She took out the key from her old pair of shorts and put it in the zipped pocket of her clean pair. Grace ran downstairs with her trainers in her hands, jumping the final couple of steps. Grace listened to the commentator on the TV reporting how the first Euros tournament game had broken records with a sell-out stadium, and how wonderful the goal was that had clinched the win.

"I'll watch the game later," Grace said as she chewed on her hash browns and baked beans. "I've promised Beth I'll play football again."

"I hope you're not playing too much football now the season is over." Dad was starting to get concerned.

"No, no! It's fun." Grace smiled, and with that she put on her trainers, rinsed her mouth with orange juice and said goodbye to everyone. Even Benjamin sat and stared at his sister, wondering where she got all her energy from!

Outside the front door Beth was sat on the wall, looking at her latest packet of Euro stickers, waiting for Grace to appear.

"Hi, you OK? All set?" Grace asked with a beaming smile.

"Yes. I am a little nervous, though," Beth replied.

"Don't worry, I was nervous to begin with. I'm here. You will be fine!" Grace gave a reassuring squeeze on Beth's arm as they started to walk down the road to the park.

"I was so tired after yesterday I missed the Lionesses game!" Grace started to say, as the pace of walking towards the park got quicker. "I will watch it later. Did you watch it?" continued Grace.

"No, I was tired too," replied Beth. "We could watch it together!"

It was unusually quiet at the park with a single dog walker, and the coffee hut was open.

"I'm going to get a couple of bottles of water before we start. We always need to keep hydrated," said Grace.

Grace paid for the drinks and handed one of the bottles to Beth as they walked towards the pitch. They sat down inside the centre circle, just inside the worn chalk lines. The girls began to talk about their plan.

"Right, whenever I take out the key it shows colours and sparks, and it shimmers. Then the goal does the same, and after a few seconds I see a door. I put the key in and turn the key twice and it opens. Then I go through," explained Grace.

Beth took a sip from her water bottle as her mouth was dry from her nervousness. "Where do you think we will end up, Grace?" asked Beth.

"No idea! It's always a surprise," answered Grace. Grace and Beth finished off their drinks, and Grace took the key from her pocket. The girls looked at the key and looked closely at the finer detail of the football boot.

After a while the key began to wobble and sparkle and shimmer, as the girls thought it would. The key let off white and red sparks and a shimmering light. The girls jumped up and looked at the goals at each end of the pitch, wondering which way they would need to go. Nothing happened. The girls waited longer, jogging to one of the goals, and then standing and staring at the other.

"Oh look!" Beth piped up, pointing at the goal at the other end of the pitch. The girls just stood in awe of the goal which was now shimmering red and white. The posts and the crossbar of the goal had now turned into an archway, with three lions jumping over the arch.

"You know what, Beth? That arch looks a bit like the Wembley arch!" Grace stood looking at the goal and the girls started to walk towards it.

Within the goal stood a tower with a lock attached. The tower looked like a castle turret and next to that there was a second one, stood like its identical twin. Grace put the key in and Beth put her hand over Grace's to help turn the key.

After turning the key twice, the door to the tower opened. Holding hands, the two girls went into the tower underneath the famous Wembley arch and they both disappeared.

10

Arriving at Wembley – the final

The firework smoke slowly disappeared, and Grace found herself standing again on a red carpet, sandwiched between two football players. She could see on their white shirts that their names were Ellen White and Fran Kirby. As the national anthem began to play, Grace looked over at the dugout and could see Beth standing with Beth England and Nikita Parris.

Leah Williamson and the German captain went to the referee who tossed the coin to decide which end the teams would attack. They swapped crests and got ready for the game. Grace was ready to start the game in place of an England player who had become sick during the team talk. The ball was delivered and was placed by the referee onto the centre spot. All the players were in position as an all-woman fly-past happened overhead. Grace stared up to the sky in awe of the planes as they flew over.

Grace waited with her right foot on the ball. The whistle blew and the game began. Grace kicked off, passing the ball to Millie Bright who kicked the ball long downfield. Grace started a run towards their attacking goal. The ball flew over the head of White, and Grace saw the ball being picked up by a Germany player who kicked the ball over everyone's head. It reached Rachel Daly who passed back to Mary Earps, the England goalkeeper.

"Settle down," screamed Earps as she waited for everyone to get back into position.

Grace took a long breath in and then out. Grace turned and waited for the game to start again. Earps passed the ball to Bright, who passed it to Beth Mead. However, it was too far and went out for a Germany throw.

With a gap in play, Grace looked around at her surroundings. Over 87,000 people had turned out for the match. She could smell the faint firework smoke. There were people young and old watching the game, all draped in white and red. *The colours look just like the key,* thought Grace.

The game restarted. Kirby took the ball and passed back to Bright who passed to Daly. Daly kicked the ball long towards Grace. Grace ran the length of the pitch, a skill she was known for in training at Oaktree Fields FC. A German player tackled and the ball went out for an England throw.

Daly threw the ball on, and Grace headed it towards the goal the team were attacking. Grace started a good run of possession. The ball came back wide for Grace. *I'm going to cross the ball into the box. We need to score,* Grace quickly thought, knowing every touch or header of the ball was important. Unfortunately, the ball was picked up by the German goalkeeper, but with pressure from the other forward in Grace's team.

This is a quick game, thought Grace. Grace knew that any slips or a moment of distraction and the opposition would take advantage and goals would be scored. "We've started really well. Keep going!" shouted Grace.

Grace went for a run to keep the pressure on the opposition. Grace got the ball and kicked it long towards the goalkeeper, but the goalkeeper got her fingertips to it and it went behind the goal for a corner. The corner was quickly taken, and Grace jumped high for it and headed the ball towards goal. There were lots of players around the goal, and somehow the German goalkeeper got the ball in her hands and fell to the ground. Everyone ran back to their positions and waited for the goalkeeper to release the ball. The ball came to Grace who swiftly passed the ball to Keira Walsh, but then the whistle blew for half-time. The score was still 0–0.

Grace took a sip of water from her water bottle, which had her name written in gold along the side. Grace heard lots of chatter but couldn't make out any of the words as everyone spoke at once. There was sudden order when the head coach spoke calmly and confidently:

"Keep possession. Do everything we have talked about. Let's continue to inspire the nation!"

The whole team got into a circle and Ella Toone grabbed Grace's hand. All hands were in the middle. "Team!" shouted the players, raising their hands from the middle into the air. They all left the dressing room to line up ready to return to the pitch.

The second half started as the first had finished, with lots of possession from both teams, and each team doing untimely tackles with some resulting in yellow cards. Grace kept playing, living her best life and playing her best football.

Lucy Bronze put in a tackle and got the ball. She started to weave in and out of the opposition. She passed to Walsh who passed the ball to Grace.

Grace then chipped the ball over the German defence and goalkeeper, and the ball ended up at the back of the net. Grace waited to see if there will be an offside flag or a VAR check, but nothing came. Grace ran, shouting, and jumped on to her teammates who congratulated her.

"You did it! Amazing goal!" Bronze said to Grace.

"Come on! We can do this!" shouted Grace over the noise of the thousands in the stadium.

It was now 1–0 to England. Germany took the restart kick quickly, giving Grace very little time to catch her breath. Germany had lots of possession and they wanted to equalise. The ball was played out to the German wing. The cross came in, and the German forward, only a few feet away from the goalline, punted the ball into the back of the net. 1–1.

Grace collected the ball from the goal net and, with it under one arm, she ran back to the centre circle. This time England quickly took the restart. Grace passed the ball to Walsh, and off they went. With 10 minutes to go Grace and the other 21 players were getting tired. *What would Sam say?* pondered Grace. *Keep going and never give up!* Grace's legs were starting to get heavy, and time for a winning goal was running out. With sudden bursts of pace, Grace continued to be available, to pass and to run with the ball; being a team player!

Full-time came and the score was still 1–1, meaning extra-time; 30 minutes to decide the winner. Or would it go to penalties, and would England's history of penalty-taking against Germany conclude the game again? The two teams stayed out on the side of the pitch close to the dugouts. Drinks were handed out, and Grace and the team crowded around the head coach. The head coach spoke wise words to each player. Grace felt the team's togetherness, and everyone was focused. The team gave a round of applause which some would think was the end of the performance, but Grace knew it was a sign to the rest of the team that the players were there, they understood what they heard, and promised to honour what was said. Lots of encouragement echoed around the circle – the England team's bubble.

"We've got this!" shouted Grace as she felt the pocket that held her magic key, making sure it was still, there playing its part in the game as it always did.

The two captains and the refereeing team met at the centre circle again to toss the coin and agree on which direction the teams would kick off the extra-time. Germany started the first 15 minutes. Germany began by passing the ball around among the team and the England players, including Grace, were doing well marking the players and pressing them. The England players got stuck in. Bronze went in for a tackle and got a free-kick from a foul. The free-kick was taken and the ball was passed along the defence, and finally a long ball reached Alessia Russo. Russo turned and off she went for a long run on the left-hand side. She passed inside to Grace who, with her first touch, half-volleyed the ball towards the goal, but the German keeper had an easy catch. Grace and the team continued to attack and defend.

The first 15 minutes ended and it was still 1–1. The teams came together at the whistle and players had enough time to take on water. Grace took sips from her water bottle. Feeling her back pocket, the key began to shake.

Back on the pitch, Grace took the ball from the referee with a thank you and placed it on the centre spot. The whistle blew. The second part of extra-time continued like the first: lots of passing, tackles, stops and starts. Grace passed the ball to Bright and it went to an England midfield player. England played some clever football. A German substitute came on with a piece of paper and tried to show her teammate what was on it. Grace, being her cheeky self, looked over the player's shoulder at the piece of paper. It read: *Markieren Sie den brillanten spieler* (Tucker)[13]. Grace Tucker smiled a beaming smile and ran off.

---

[13] Mark the brilliant forward

Grace got hold of a poor German pass and quickly passed to Russo who then passed it back to Grace. Grace chipped the ball onto Chloe Kelly who ran into the six-yard box. She kicked the ball along the ground through the legs of the defender and it crossed the goalline. 2–1 to England. Kelly ran over to Grace and they hugged.

"A great goal," shouted Grace to Chloe Kelly.

After more defending by England, the final whistle blew. The stadium jumped to its feet, cheering, singing and shouting; flags waving everywhere. Beth and all the players on the bench ran onto the pitch shouting, and started jumping onto their teammates and hugging them. The England team shook the German players' hands. The Germans were sad so Grace went over to some of the players she had played with before and said, "Well done, you played very well," and gave them a hug.

The celebrations began, and the medals, the player of the tournament and the golden boot trophies were handed out. Then the tournament trophy was handed to Williamson. Grace and Beth walked away from the rest of the team. They reached the centre circle and Grace took out the key. Grace, feeling tired, lay down and Beth sat down beside her, both looking above at the evening sky broken by the Wembley arch. Meanwhile, everyone was dancing and singing with the England team. Grace rubbed the grass from the key and the friends disappeared.

Grace and Beth walked with a little skip of joy from the park back to Grace's house. Grace knocked on the front door and Mum answered. "You two look like you've had a good game," Mum said.

They went into the kitchen and Grace poured two glasses of apple juice, giving one to Beth. They went into the front room, turned on the TV and just fell into the seats.

"Oh, I thought I heard the front door," said Dad as he peeped around the front room. "And just the two I'm looking for," continued Dad as he walked further into the room and placed something onto the coffee table. "Here is a gift for the pair of you, for playing a fantastic season and attending all the training sessions.

By the way, I'm taking you!" finished Dad, and he walked out the room. (But he only went so far so he could still hear and see what would happen next.)

Grace and Beth looked at the thin white envelope that Dad had placed onto the table. Grace took the envelope and both girls quickly sat up. Grace opened the envelope.

"It's tickets to the Euro tournament Final!" shouted Grace.

Grace showed Beth, and they both jumped up and started bouncing up and down and hugging each other. Suddenly they stopped, and Grace and Beth looked at the tickets again. "Wow! This is amazing!" shouted Grace. "We're going to Wembley and it's going to be brilliant" continued Grace.

"Wow, amazing! I can't wait. It's going to be great!" said an excited Beth.

"Thanks, Dad," shouted Grace.

"Thanks, Mr Tucker! It's an amazing surprise. We can't wait!" beamed Beth.

"England just need to progress well in the tournament," smiled Grace.

"They can do it!" gleamed Beth.

For the last time, Grace unzipped the pocket of her shorts and took out the key. Both Grace and Beth looked at the rusty old key. Suddenly, the key began to shake and change. One side– the piece that goes into the lock– gradually changed into a leaf shape and the other changed to what looked like the shape of a kangaroo.

"What does this mean, Grace?" asked Beth.

Grace and Beth stood by the front room windows to better see.

"I think it might mean we are going to New Zealand and Australia, Beth. They are symbols from those countries. And you know what's happening over there..."

"The World Cup!" shouted Grace and Beth, and with that they gave each other a hug. Grace looked out the front window and could see Lottie with her grandma standing across the road getting ready to get into a car.

"That's Sue Lopez!" said Grace. The two girls stopped hugging and knocked on the window hard to get their attention. Finally, they waved at Lottie, Lottie's grandma and Sue. Grace used the key to wave. Sue looked across the road and, with a beaming smile, waved back.

11

The history of England's women's football

1894   Dick, Kerr Ladies is formed in Preston.

1921   Women's football banned from Football league grounds.

1971   FA lift the ban.

1972   First women's international game in Britain.

1991   WFA launch a national league. 24 clubs join.

1994   The league is known as the Women's Premier League.

2005   England hosts the UEFA Women's Championship.

2011	FA Women's Super League begins.
2014	England women play their first match at Wembley Stadium.
2015	England win bronze at FIFA Women's World Cup in Canada.
2017	England reach the semi-finals of UEFA Euros.
2019	England win the SheBelieves Cup.
2022	England win UEFA Euros tournament in front of over 87,000 (stadium) and 17 million watching on TV.

About the Author

Emma was born and lives in Salisbury, Wiltshire. When she was young, she played one game for Salisbury Girls and many games with her dad and brother. She watched her local non-league football team for 20 years.

Emma was a primary teacher until the COVID pandemic in 2020 when she began her 2nd Masters degree which is in Children's Literature and was inspired by this course to start writing.

In her spare time, Emma enjoys watching sport, especially football. Also spending time running and walking in support for charities close to her heart.